I0525456

Ps-Fs: Prompts and Fictions

A Collection of Shorts

Sunil Sharma

SETU PUBLICATIONS
Pittsburgh, USA

Ps-Fs: Prompts and Fictions
A Collection of Shorts

By
Sunil Sharma

Setu Publications
* Pittsburgh, PA (USA) *

© 2019 by Sunil Sharma

All rights reserved. No part of this work may be reproduced, translated, recorded, stored, transmitted, or displayed in any form, or by any means electronic, mechanical, or otherwise without the prior written permission of the author, the copyright owner except for brief quotations in book reviews, and as otherwise permitted by applicable law. Any such quotations must acknowledge the source.

We would be pleased to receive email correspondence regarding this publication or related topics at **setuedit@gmail.com**.

ISBN-13 (paperback): 978-1-947403-04-8

Printed and bound in the United States of America.

Distributed to the book trade worldwide by Setu Publications, Pittsburgh (USA)

Although every precaution has been taken in the preparation of this work, neither the author nor the publisher shall have any liability to any person or entity with respect to any loss or damage caused or alleged to be caused directly or indirectly by the information contained in this work.

Setu Literary Publications, Pittsburgh, USA

Ps-Fs

(Prompts and Fictions)

A COLLECTION OF SHORTS

BY SUNIL SHARMA

Preface: The Ps-Fs

It is with much pleasure that I write this preface to Sunil Sharma's latest collection of short stories called the Ps-Fs: Prompts and Fictions. Flash, short and slightly longer fiction works have been carefully selected to transport the reader to magical realms, distant lands, local Indian realities of day-to-day life, and the emotional centre of the heart.

As I mentioned in my review of Sunil's most recent book of poetry (*Interactions*), by collecting his literary gems into one volume allows readers to peruse the works at their leisure rather than feeling pressurised, when reading online, screen- based publications. All the stories in this book have been published online at Mercurial Press, the short stories have a limit of five-hundred words; the longer ones, one or two thousand words. A further imposed restraint is that the stories must be written in a specific time-period, five days or so, for five hundred words, and fifteen days for the longer ones. These constraints help get the authors "creative juices flowing".

It matters not whether Sunil is writing poetry or fiction, as all of his literary output, which is prolific, is underpinned by a "liberal humanism". Liberal humanism recognises that all humans regardless of class, race, gender, age, religious beliefs, and position in society are equally important. It is an ethical system that recognises human dignity as of vital importance, not over and above nature, but together with and part of the totality of existence. In his own words; *"That liberal-humanism and commitment for the downtrodden still forms my inner vision and overall outlook on life and informs my writing."*

The stories in this collection are characterised by the use of ordinary, day-to-day language. He avoids and dislikes intellectualism and literary formalism as an end in itself. One of the Golden Rules of good writing is, it should not draw attention to the writing itself, but take the reader on an immersive, inner journey. Sunil does this very well, often leaving the reader with a tear in their eye!

Acts of kindness and goodness are all around us, if we care to look, sometimes this callous, brutal world masks these acts. However, Sunil's unique ability to juxtapose good and bad, meanness and charity, despair and hope gives his fiction, a very special quality. It was this quality that connected me with Sunil many years ago; the first poem of his I read still resonates with empathy in my mind. I also often think of some character from one of his stories whose actions or plight is indelible in my mind; to me, no higher quality of literature can surpass this kind of impact. Beware dear reader, you are about to be enchanted too.

The book is nicely produced, published by the USA-based Setu Publications, and runs to over 100 pages. There are twenty nine stories of varying length; one of my most favourite stories is *The Clown That Was Not*, oh what an ending!

Sunil Sharma lives in the teeming metropolis of Mumbai, India. He is a college principal and has published 20 books, joint and solo. The works include well-received anthologies of fiction and poetry, critical and literary, journal articles and his own volumes of poetry. He has been influenced by many writers such as Dickens, Tolstoy, Chekov, Camus, Marquez, Kafka and Prem Chand but it is Gorky who is his main inspiration.

Short fiction seems to be experiencing somewhat of a renaissance. This volume of stories goes a long way in bringing this vital literary genre before the public to both enjoy and to uplift our post-postmodern jaded spirits.

Robert Maddox-Harle,
Artist and author
Lismore,
Australia

First Person Singular: Ps-Fs
(Prompts and Fictions)

These are 29 short stories, published by the *Mercurial Stories*.

A challenge to write, as these are inspired by a prompt and a time limit.

Writing to prompts is becoming popular assignment. Many journals send out tentative ideas and expect artistic imagination to get inspired and kicking. Different from your usual inspiration sources---a critical moment or mood; an appealing face or scene witnessed by a creative mind, restive; actively registering the mundane and the resultant interaction producing some concrete imagery and perhaps, a credible ending with a subtle message hidden somewhere in the dynamic text.

Writing fiction is a difficult art. It involves intensity, hard work and few sittings. Poetry is shorter and can be done quickly as compared with the short fiction. Under the genre of free verse, any random assemblage of words can be safely termed as poetry.

Writing Prompts and Fictions---flash or micro or long piece---demands another kind of mindset and intense labor. One has to mold the imagination to the given theme, usually a one-liner, tentative, tantalizing, and, working around that elusive idea with the tools of the field invariably involves patience and regular practice. And, of course, craft. A scene-setting; dialogues; characters; conflict and a finale that is convincing and logical, internally and externally, for the well-read reader ready to invest in that work. It is called "relatable" these days---the fiction thus created in and for an age in a hurry. If it is not, the loss of interest is bound to follow. Another thing is that everything is getting micro now, including human patience and attention-span. In the clutter, the finished product must stand out. But content is the real driver. Even a market blitz can flounder in the long run, if content fails. Best sellers of last year look so trite in this year.

A writer has to compete on many parameters.

A huge and daunting job for a poor, unpaid and unrecognized word-player!

Also, a labor of love, writing fiction, long or short!

Oddly enough, fictions reveal truths and new realms.

These flashes do that only.

Hope you enjoy these works of fiction that I call Ps-Fs: Prompts and Fictions. I am indebted to the editor, *Merculiar Stories* (Credit: https://mercurialstories.com) for giving them due space, along with other writers.

Gratitude to:

The eminent artist and author from Australia, Rob Harle, for writing an overview of these published stories in his wonderful *Preface*.

Anurag Sharma, the reputed editor-in-chief and publisher and CEO of *Setu* journal, for his support and faith in humble me by bringing out the collection of shorts, as a book, my third one in total and first one by the USA-based Setu Publications, Pittsburgh, USA.

Dear reader, enter the world of the real through the imagined fictional!

Sunil Sharma,
Mumbai,
India
July 31, 2019

Ps-Fs: Contents

MONDAY BLUES AND AFTER

Generally, it happens on Fridays—the late-afternoon chat with the boss over tepid coffee; some common topics and then, the pink slip given without warning—a Tyson punch that knocks the wind out of the hit.
Hurried goodbyes. Silent tears!

For him, it happened on Monday.

Morning he was in the job. By 5 pm—out!

As in a tragedy, he could not believe this happening to him.

Why me? He asked the gods, quiet as usual.

Devastated, he went to the Marine Lines and watched a rain-soaked Mumbai skyline.

Lights came on, giving the place a magical feel.

The murky waters of a choppy sea beckoned as a solution to all the existential blues.

He sat dangling over the sea wall and thought of his options. At 38, no job; piling house -loan arrears; medicine bills; tuition fees; groceries.

Jumping into the sea was a temptation…

—Saar!

He looked back.

A kid selling roasted grams—eyes and tone pleading; frail body in faded clothes; tousled hair.

He dismissed the child with a rude gesture.

—Saar!

The voice was grating.

—Go away! He ordered.

—Saar! Saar! Please take a packet. Got a family to feed. Ma suffering from cancer; brother handicapped; father dead.

The tone was pleading.

—Your five rupees might get us a modest meal, Saar! I am not a beggar but a student working extra time...

The voice trailed off. The body shook. Tears mingled with the July raindrops pelting the city of glitzy bars, hotels and offices.

The downsized man looked into the eyes of the child, sobbing loudly—and oddly, saw his own kid in that gaunt face.

And felt terrified!

—Any elders left in family? He asked.

—Two elder brothers.

—They not supporting?

The kid paused. Then: The eldest separated long ago with his family. Second brother ran away.

Shocked, the man asked: You too can also run away?

The kid took a long breath.

—Running is not an option for some, Saar.

The man was struck dumb!

Everything changed fast afterwards.

He fished out a ten rupee note, patted the boy and said: Keep on fighting. Those down will rise up one day in life!

A message by a father to a migrant son trying to find work and shelter in Mumbai—recalled suddenly and relayed to another struggler.

The boy smiled through the tears, mumbled a thank-you and left.

Then he got a visual on phone, sent perhaps by a divine design: Sisyphus riding up the mountain with his burden.

Revived, he picked up his bag and bid goodbye to the murky depths.

—Where are you?

WhatsApp query.

—Starting over again…he wrote back, smiling at the world in general.

A SUMMER NIGHT AND BUTTERFLIES

That you have but slumbered here
While these visions did appear.
—Shakespeare

Summer nights are magical. This being one. That familiar smell: *Raat Rani*!

Startled, he becomes fully awake. *No Queen of Night in the Mumbai home!*

Odd! The fragrance lingers strongly… triggering a sensation.

A crevice opens up:

… Ma grew the night-blooming jasmine that rendered long summer nights aromatic. He would fall asleep by the scent wafting up to the roof where the family slept, watching the moon-uncle and the stars, the divine bodies so near, yet so far; the experience, almost other-worldly.

… father talking of fairies, Puck, enchanted forest… to a pale and diffident kid…with a stammer and low self-esteem; a dreamer, academically poor during those magical hot nights under a North Indian sky; often, in the distance, thunder and light, creating regions fantastic…now lost forever.

Restive, he gets up and throws open the windows on the smoggy city.

Urban sounds rush in.

…a long train-whistle: Instantly, taking him back to a provincial town. Elder brother leaving for an army post in Kashmir; a tearful good-bye…the dreadful news…killed in action…

Something died that day along with the martyr.

Subsequently, he left for Mumbai and forgot the delightful summers that kept them awake as a family and enjoy the bounties of sky and earth. Folks talking into mid-night, lying down on the stringed cots, fanned by a hot breeze, contented, simple, un-complaining, working very hard, believing in a just God. Cool mornings would come as a pleasant surprise.

The whole neighborhood slept in the open—the way passengers still sleep on the platform of a railway terminus, long lines of people with hands and legs tucked in, like packed statues—a community of underdogs united by adversity and finer values and empathy.

They were all one extended family—localities, communities and cities—all one. That innocence is lost in 2018.

As the night advances, he hears other sounds— The Nepali cook stir-frying noodles in the corner joint; the thud-thud amplified by the comparative quiet of street, getting emptier.

Crescendo of harsh decibels: ear-splitting horns; strays barking madly; a siren in a distant alley; somebody talking loudly on phone.

As the silvery light brightens the jagged skyline, he remembers another sepia-tinted scene, from a different age.

The catching of fireflies on the special summer nights—an interesting activity:

...they would go with nets and jars. The gloom would be illuminated by these fascinating creatures. A strange glow in the dark fields; dots punctuating the sheet of liquid blackness. Kids and adults catching the moths in jars and nets in fields and forests. The nightly expedition, liberating, exhilarating, giving a high; an encounter with nature outdoors, so re-vitalizing!

As Raghav, the busy screen-play writer, stares at the unwinding streets, he smiles at the childhood and early youth coming back and reviving the clogged arteries and innards, due to heavy schedule.

I wish I could chase butterflies in Mumbai, every summer night!

MEMORIES OF A SMALL TOWN

Maxim Gorky in north India!

Back then, Ghaziabad was liberal and art loving. Tree-lined roads; quaint bungalows; big parks; schools, colleges and hospitals—an ideal address.

It was *his* hometown—neat, ordered, tranquil, educated, liberal, middle class.

And truly cosmopolitan.

On that evening, returning home, he found a solitary bookshop on the Station Road. And the Master there!

His life-long tryst with the Russians began that instant. Every fortnight, the young man would trudge there for a Pushkin, Gogol or Chekov. Gave tuitions, saved money for the classics; hard cover and well-produced, yet affordable for a lower-middle-class student, doing an M.A in English.

Exhilarating encounter!

The shop slowly became a magnet for the enthusiasts: over cups of *chai*, debates over the Immortals and comparisons with the French and the English were conducted. The translated books in Hindi and English, mainly from Russia, were displayed there, along with some Hindi magazines and stationery items. The owner was a failed writer and wanted to make a living by selling literature of a foreign country in a dusty town, 28 km away from Delhi, the Capital of a post-colonial country.

The literate town did not disappoint the bookseller.

Ghaziabad was getting urbanized and industrialized fast in the 1990s. A bunch of idealists tried surviving in that bleak space by staging a Brecht and/or holding poetry sessions, Ghazal evenings, painting exhibitions, some place or other.

It was pure oxygen!

The initiates would discuss Kurosawa, Ray, Fellini or Osborne.

Often, international film shows were held through a film club; being artist was bliss for the out-of-the- job dreamers, young rebels!

A lean and intense man, Raghav Verma was deeply attached to *his* town: Still small— every street, face and café, familiar. Neighbors=family. People smiled at the strangers.

Inclusive!

Comfortable zone!

You truly *belonged* there.

... death of Pa altered things forever. He had to seek a job. The town suddenly grew very small and stifling! No opportunities. He bid a teary farewell to a place whose winds and waters had nourished a yearning soul and body...akin to bidding goodbye to a poor mother!

Reality sank in. He left for Mumbai in the late 1990s and found a calling as a screen- play writer. He got money and recognition in a mega city of million aspirations.

Ghaziabad became a receding landscape. A different age!

...

On a recent visit in 2018, after more than a decade, he found his hometown transmogrified!

Ghaziabad had grown heavy and ugly. The old lanes brimmed with shops. Each street was a mini-market. Malls, multiplexes, bars.

Ghaziabad— an open *bazaar*. Fancy cars. Bikes. Pizza and Big Mac outlets. Beauty- massage parlours.

Shocking!

Where is *his* Ghaziabad?

Small becoming big; big, bigger; a mad race!

He searched for old cultural landmarks—the bookshop, old cafés, theatres.

Nothing.

Ads of deep discounts; happy hours and sales, in every corner; everything was on sale.

Sadly, Gorky has been exiled by Porsche… forever!

THE GAME

They were the dreaded RASUB!

And tough to crack!

.

Post-lunch, the ritual started.

The man called God ordered: Proceed!

The second man, identified as Charles Ludwig Dodgson, intoned: KO.

The third man, Homer and the fourth, Nietzsche, repeated: KO.

The hymn KO-KO reverberated across the hall and corridor.

.

The director was aghast.

—What the hell!

—Watch for few more minutes, sir!

The deputy pleaded.

.

KO.

KO.

KO.

KO.

The director was incensed: Sheer nonsense!

—A daily game!

—Find out the *meaning* of this drivel! Some real conspiracy here! Find out.

—Yes, sir.

.

The group was given third-degree. The interrogators insisted for the *hidden* meaning.

The frail victims shouted: KOKOKO!!!

—What does KO mean? The chief asked.

—Key O— Kcy O   Key O— KO-KO!

—What does it mean?

—*When I use a word, it means just what I choose it to mean — neither more nor less.*

—*Which is to be master...*

The interrogators gave up.

.

The inmates were intellectuals feared for their theories that altered perceptions and critiqued the System.

Part of a shrinking movement called RASUB—some got murdered; others disappeared or shot down; many died in

jails—these four minds were committed to the safest haven—
the Asylum—by declaring them as mad.

They were the enemies—for claiming that everybody was
divine and therefore equal.

The State did not like such a philosophy.

It was the job of the director to eliminate threats.

Non-sense is subversive!

That was official decree.

.

The group kept on chanting: KO. KO.KO.

The director and his team were driven nuts.

They could not make sense of the chant. The Director brought
in specialist that worked hard to understand the game but
miserably failed.

The more the four were tortured, the fiercer the recital: KO-KO.

As if their sanity depended on this mantra!

.

The Home Department sent the ultimatum: Three days to
unravel the *meaning*!

On the brink, the portly director joined the group in disguise—
for better understanding of their world and mental processes.

God said: Proceed!

Dodgson said: KO.

The director said: KO.

They all stood up, linked arms, closed eyes and started dancing as initiates in the mysteries.

God said: They can kill body, not mind!

Others shouted: KO.

God said: They can kill minds, not thoughts!

The group shouted: KO.

God said: We are all one. We all are God!

Blasphemy! Thought the Director.

God sang the loudest:

They can maim us

But not our spirit

And— not our songs

That defy time!

Superman: KO! KO! KO!

They all chorused: KOKOKOKO! KOKOKO!

God: Next?

Dodgson: NUF!

Nietzsche: Finnegan and Jabberwocky! Godot.

Dodgson: Love math, time travel. Back from 1865.

The director recommended: Commit them to the dungeons.
Saboteurs and their verbal games—lethal!

Lastly: TEL METH TOR! They are *GO-GAUG*— advanced
creative people, best understood in future only!

He was also put in that hell!

FRAGMENT FROM THE YELLOW DIARY

.

Adore yellow—reminds me of turmeric.

Of the Arles *Sunflowers*.

Of *The Yellow House* (The Street), 1888.

.

Vincent wanted to create a symphony of yellow and blue. He claimed sunflowers as his own.

I love Vincent.

Therefore, I, too, love these tender flowers that got the great artist's special attention, in two series, and made them iconic across the world.

Whatever Vincent touched became gold.

Posthumously.

Shameful!

The painter died pauper, unsung.

Fate of a true artist.

Now— enjoys cult following.

.

Yellow.

Melancholic—like a wintry afternoon.

Magical also: The Yellow House is a landmark for fans. Vincent wanted to create a studio of the south where painters could live and work in a shared space. Gauguin was there as guest but things went from good to bad.

Rest is history.

Yellow House where a genius lived for short time. Resented by neighbors.

They found him a threat and wanted him to be sent to an asylum.

An artist as a *threat*!

Every great artist is a danger.

Society does not want them outside but inside a nut house, every age.

How funny!

Who is sane?

The bourgeois?

Or Gogh?

.

Why is yellow appealing?

Is it its lightness?

Or ability to blend?

Both.

It sits soothingly—on eyes and mind.

That is why a disturbed Vincent employed the yellow and rendered it vividly.

And made it famous as a medium.

.

Yellow signals jaundice.

Death. Decay.

Friendship.

A primary color.

Have seen many dead with pale faces.

The face drained of color—except an odd paleness that confirms lack of vitality, breath, life.

The paleness found on Vincent's hollow face.

Perhaps, he was living and dying at the same instant—like an autumn evening.

.

In India, the weddings are incomplete sans turmeric (*haldi* in Hindi) application—the lotion applied to both the bride and groom. Called *Haldirasam*, this ritual takes hours and involves cleansing amidst song and dance by the family in a room. After bath, it leaves the body resplendent.

The spectrum of yellow!

Fire is yellow. It too cleanses base material and purifies.

Baptism through fire.

·

I call my diary, a yellow diary.

It contains smudges of turmeric on the first and last pages.

Have drawn yellow lines across few pages.

Yellow and white background mix together and create a stunning visual.

Try that.

You will find your inner Vincent through such elementary sketching, doodling and drawing.

Art is about creating new patterns, visuals, artifacts, verbal objects.

By drawing a yellow line across a white art-sheet, I am trying to do a Vincent—and trying to understand his mental state in that Yellow House.

These few entries on August 16 of 2018 at 5.30 pm, in Mumbai, are random attempts at capturing the flux of that state.

And tribute to *Sunflowers* and *The Yellow House* that brought out the best and worst in a creative mind, mostly misunderstood in his lifetime!

Perhaps, it was meant to end like that only.

Masks— a room full of them!

—How are you?

I turned around to face a mask facing me.

—What is that?

—The Noh-men or *Omote*.

Replied Harsh, my ad-hoc host.

—Got a big collection.

—Yeah.

He removed the mask: Welcome home, buddy!

—Thanks.

I replied.

—You keep on surprising.

I added.

—Well, the collection is worth three lakhs.

He said. I nodded.

—Harsh is crazy!

An announcement in a female voice.

—Meet your new sister-in-law, Smita, crazier than me.

We shook hands. Moved to the sea-facing balcony.

—How is the view? Harsh asked.

—Nice!

—Hmm! Nice! *Yaar*, it is spectacular! Worth 15 crores, this 24th-floor house in this part of the vertical Mumbai.

A waiter poured drinks. The sun-set indeed looked beautiful!

—Not for me. I do not drink.

I said.

—Come on! A French import. Cost me a fortune. A bit?

—No thanks.

—Your loss!

They both sipped.

—How is life?

Harsh asked.

—Going on.

—Where you live?

Smita queried.

—Virar.

—Never heard about that place.

She shrugged haughtily.

—You are lucky.

I said. She remained grim, playing with her diamond ring.

—So, what is going on?

Harsh again.

—As usual. Nothing exciting. You?

—Lots of excitement. A model as a wife. Wonderful kids. Going abroad for three-week vacation.

I smiled.

—Are you still there?

He asked.

—Yes.

—Want to join my start-up?

I said nothing.

—Manage that. Will pay five times more—for old times' sake. And a car and chauffeur to drive you around in the city.

I kept mum.

—Think over. Do not get stuck in that hell-hole for life. Move up—as I did.

I nodded.

—Not many old friends would make such a life-changing offer.

I smiled. Smita looked at my workday clothes and rolled her eyes.

—That is why I called you up for this meeting. A big offer for my old friend.

Just then, my cell rang.

—Boss calling!

I went inside the huge hall where different masks stared at me from varied angles. After I finished, I made for the balcony—that wide deck full of flowers and a privileged view of the city-sprawl.

Her voice made me stop.

—Why?

I felt like becoming a fly-on-the-wall. Fixed—listening.

The voices grew louder. Smita's tone was high. His, subdued.

—We go a long way, hon. His father was my father's chum. Come from the same Kolkata. We spent college days together.

—So?

—Try to understand, hon.

—You try to understand, dear Harsh. Not *worth* our time and money.

—I know. He is not worth but we need honest guys…

A mask swayed in the sea-breeze.

Then others began dancing—frantically.

And an Oni mask fell off before me.

THE LAST ROMANTIC

As soon as he rushed into the compartment, breathless and disoriented, the train began moving across Vienna that looked different: A certain melancholia that attends the intersection of dusk and an advancing night.

Evening: In-between space characterized by a sublime mix of mellow darkness and dying light— divine works in chiaroscuro.

Forlorn and lost.

From the window- seat, he could feel the overpowering sadness of the hour. The offices were getting empty and streets filled up—fast.

Close!

Few seconds late and he would have missed the connection to Paris!

Once settled, he found *her* opposite.

Their eyes met and diverted—at the same time.

What quickly registered were a freckled face; the goggles on a dishevelled head and an aloofness, typical of the solo female tourists.

That demeanour, oddly, was fascinating!

There were others. An Italian family—boisterous, chatty, loud—reminded of his family. The remaining travellers were on another planet—plugged into phones or lap tops.

He took out the book.

—Ayn Rand?

He looked up—into the smiling eyes of his co-passenger.

—Do you take Middle Eastern males to be savages?

She replied: No offense, please. Just curious.

The lilting tone soothed.

—Fine. No offense, either.

They relaxed.

—I am Anne. Freelance travel writer. Boston.

—David here. Manager. Berlin.

The strangers shook hands. Train hurtled down.

—Travelling Paris? She asked.

—Yes. You? He asked for the sake of conversation.

—Yes. Doing a piece on Paris and Multi-cultural Perspectives.

—Cool!

—Your first visit?

—No. Come often. You?

— I, too, keep on returning. Paris beckons as a besotted lover. You cannot resist Paris.

He nodded.

She continued: Ayn Rand in the summer of 2018 is a revelation...

—That too in the hands of an Arab.

She smiled: Not that implication. Ayn Rand is not that popular these days but some iconic books have an amazing afterlife. And ways of turning up in strange places!

—Right. Once I saw Ibsen in an Indonesian village—in an old paper shop.

—Yes. I once saw Thoreau in a Shanghai house of a factory worker, dreaming of a passage to America.

—Globalization! He exclaimed.

—Migration and its sources of inspiration. She observed.

—In a way, border-less world, ideas travel faster and we develop standardized tastes.

—Yeah. We are all Potter fans. Believers in magic. Fantasy sells.

He nodded: Yes. Books can change beliefs.

—So does travel.

They talked best-sellers and movies and found a lot in common.

—Travel often? He asked.

—Yes.

—Escaping America.

—Hmm! Maybe. She said.

—Or searching for the nirvana?

—Perhaps. You? Searching the Exotic Paris?

He smiled: Searching for the soul of the city that once hosted Joyce and Proust.

She was floored: You are highly cultivated!

—A dark prince! A Moor?

She won his heart by that dimpled smile!

.

They reached Paris late as the train got held up due to some technical problem. Decided to spend more time together by exploring the nightly life. Crowds everywhere. The sidewalk cafes were full. They drank the best wine, ate dinner and leisurely walked down the river-front, enjoying the breeze and the spectacular scene. The Seine reflected the lights. Every nationality could be seen there on the boulevards.

Another world!

Paris, the truly cosmopolitan!

—Certain things are fated. David said, holding her hands, on the bench, near a bridge.

—Indeed. Never thought I would have you as a companion!

He smiled: Frankly, I took you for a snobbish Yankee.

She was equally frank: I took you for a boorish Moor.

They both laughed.

—We have destroyed the power of stereotypes. Said David.

—Thanks to Ayn Rand and Paris. Anne said and added: Paris can cast spell on folks belonging to different cultures and make strangers into friends. Paris is heavenly!

—Yes. The cities can be mysterious. Deep South, such things are not possible. David said.

After a long silence, David said: There are strong coincidences. I cannot believe such things happening. But here we are—the Moor and his princess, in this city of love and romance, on a pleasant night, along a beautiful river. This is magical!

—Yes. Anne said, in Paris only, odd things can happen. The city has its own enchantment and can dissolve barriers. This mood can be best summed up by the immortal Rumi: This is love: to fly toward a secret sky, to cause a hundred veils to fall each moment. First to let go of life.Finally, to take a step without feet.

David went lyrical:

For you, in my respect, are all the world.
Then how can it be said I am alone
When all the world is here to look on me?

Anne said; Indeed! A midsummer night's dream coming true for us, the ones chosen by Cupid on this lovely night.So bizarre, yet true.Fated, perhaps.

David beamed. I am a hard-core Romantic, last of the tribe.

—Yes, you are. Anne confirmed.

They began walking towards the shadows.

Then it happened.

The cops swooped down and arrested David who did not offer any resistance. Took him in an unmarked van. No witnesses.

.

Next morning, David was the national headline:

Top Terrorist Arrested

Paris: According to the police, the dreaded terrorist Abu Hassan has been captured. Called the Lone Bomber, he has successfully evaded arrest by assuming identities. Going by many aliases, Abu—a chemical engineer—has been on the move across the EU, the recent one being David. He is part of a fringe group that targets Western installations by planting bombs. He is the most deadly bomber, working solo, responsible for some lethal attacks in recent history. The cops are further investigating his role in other bombings. The main role in the operation was played by an undercover female agent by the name of Anne.

LESSONS

He wanted to be part of history—before becoming history.

But history is not kind: It favours only few individuals and hates the masses—the first lesson delivered by his high-school teacher that resonated so well.

Initially, he had felt cheated. Father had always insisted that it was possible to rise up in society—even for a lower-middle-class, small-town, ordinary guy, in a vibrant democracy!

Soon, he realized, he was bypassed. Grim realities caught on — lost father; dropped out; became a sales-person in a shoe shop to support a large family.

Hardly 19 at that time!

Life—raw, prosaic and brutal! Dreams belonged to another age and class.

The man who wanted to be the king became pauper, instead.

He wrote in the diary.

Selling shoes to customers was a daily challenge. Surviving on a meager salary was another existential battle.

Democracy and its promise of deliverance—a plain lie!

An epiphany recorded as a diary-entry.

.

When he turned 25 on March 25, 2018— a marginal man and doomed to be that only—somebody suggested the second best option of entering the annals—by checking the famous people or events, on that date.

Cool!

If not a general or emperor, he could bask in the reflected glory of the great.

Inder Kumar was curious to know what happened on his birthday.

After going through many such sites on his smart phone, Inder Kumar, a lean man with a perpetual hungry look, embarked on a journey backwards in time and found few incidents as most exciting, on that hot Sunday afternoon, propped up against the stacks of shoes, re-visiting memorable incidents.

.

Here, the selection:

—1199

King Richard, the Lion Heart, killed.

.

—1965

The Third Selma to Montgomery March.

.

—1811

PB Shelley rusticated from the Oxford for his easy on atheism!

.

—1957

"Howl" by Ginsberg banned!

.

—1911

The fire in Triangle Shirtwaist Factory, New York, kills 146.
.

They met in the late night.

—What did you fish out from the dustbin of history? Asked his friend Raju.

—Some fascinating facts. Said Inder.

—What kind of facts? Asked Raju.

—Random things. Made few internal connections between these occurrences separated by time and space, yet linked together, in an odd way.

—Tell me these discoveries made by a bright man, denied his greatness.

Raju did not sound sarcastic.

Inder recited the list of items culled from the belly of the past and offered his observations: That a king could be killed by a boy who is a commoner. People power can shake the well-entrenched system through a long march. Oxford and courts can ban writers on stupid reasons and continue to treat thinkers, as threats. That the poorly-paid workers can die in an inferno in an advanced democracy. Considered garbage by the capital! Yet, these disenfranchised guys made history in a modest way!

—Hmm!

—Alternative reading of events only!

THE DATE

Marriage was to be discussed over breakfast. He said even a hurricane cannot stop a Romeo!

But he never turned up. Somebody else did—and altered histories.

Here is how this Maupassant/ O' Henry- type tale unfolded in downtown Mumbai.

.

Rita occupied the window seat of *The Rendezvous*, awaiting Mr. Right, if not the Prince Charming. After a whirlwind of courtship—online exchanges; long phone chats; short meets, all compressed into a fortnight—the two decided to give it a try in the breakfast tryst. She was elated—earlier attempts at romance had failed badly, due to the increasing expectations and other norms of evaluation—commercial viability of the possible alliance; respective career trajectories; current incomes and finally, behavior towards the parents and overall gender-roles, post-marriage home. Naturally, the parties could never arrive at a consensus!

This time you will be lucky! Her flat-mate had predicted, after a peg too many. That pleased her. All the five girls—in desperate search for soul partners— wished her success. They were the only family in the megapolis.

Moved to tears!

.

As she waited for the suitor, she recalled an earlier conversation:

—Any real-time fairy-tale endings in life, granny?

—Yes, child. There are.

—The princess finding her prince, love, big castle and royalty?

—Yes.

—You never found one, ma?

The Ancient One smiled: Got a secret lover but don't disclose it to grandpa. The bearded bastard would kill!

The teen smiled and asked: How can I find true love?

—No worries, kiddo. It will find you!

She expected to find true love on that morning mission in a manic city of millions. After a long wait and unsuccessful attempts to reach him, the sad reality sank in. She was duped... again.

—Have you ever checked the mirror?

Her last boyfriend had screamed, when caught in bed with another girl. And then given the answer: Check that pug nose. The ugly specs. The uneven teeth. The coarse skin. Who would love a Ms. Plain Jane?

She took a year to recover from the hurled insults by a violent man—and then went in for a makeover with a vengeance. Blue lenses; blunt hair-style; regular bleaching and facials; long heels; trendy minis and tops—enough to make her look like a girl from London rather than provincial Ghaziabad.

Appearances can be treacherous!

As she was about to get up, in silent tears, a nerd easily slid into the opposite chair and asked in a familiar tone: You read Robbie Singh?

Offended, she countered: Why not?

—Dark fantasies?

— So what? Humans need fantasies. Inverted realities. Anticipate future—such utopias.

He declared: Genius!

—How?

—Brilliant defense of *my* best-sellers.

A stunned silence: My *ideal*! Before me!

After a long breakfast and varied discussions, she immediately grabbed the unexpected proposal: the fan and her idol to wed after three months.

Fiction never looked so real; real, fiction!

THE BARITONE

Love and its obsessions.

Narcissus transfixed with his own image.

The new-millennium world is image-driven.

Nina Ganguly, too, adored images. At 30, she was a self-declared *Alice in search of wonderland.*

She did not have to wait long.

The Alice-moment arrived, on a Sunday afternoon, in an unexpected manner.

.

Nina got electrified by a voice on the podcast.

Transported.

Entranced by quality.

The voice was like the rumbling that convulses the earth.

Strange feel and texture: Akin to the wind whispering in a remote Alpine forest, on a crisp summer morning.

Divine!

She was overwhelmed by the tenor and intensity—and its ability to move the listener to the core, the way you get enraptured, watching the Everest summit, first time.

The masculine voice triggered some long-forgotten sensation.

Jouissance—blogged thus:

...pure bliss this, like the first rain drumming on the corrugated sheets or tiles of the mud houses in the small village on the edge of the river...the big drops creating a symphony odd...the grey curtain travelling fast over the plain and the meadow, drenching the trees that dance in the strong wind...kids screaming in joy and splashing in the brown puddles, a woman singing a song in a Kolkata home, a child trying to capture the diamonds from the dark skies in outstretched hands and the manna sliding down the fingers, and, some death chant in a mourning family, the light-n-dark blending in that specific instance...

She fell in love with *it*!

She went on playing the podcast and felt uplifted.

Every time, the baritone opened up secret passages inside a heart long suspected to be cold, clogged.

A lightness of being similar to listening to Zubin Mehta or viewing *Mona Lisa*.

.

The folksy song done in a soulful voice ran:

This spring I will not be home

I will miss the beauty and the splendor

Of a rural scene

That breeze

That murmuring of bees

And waters of the river

And the song of the fishermen

And toiling boatmen

I will miss out all these

And your smile and love

Stuck up in this city of concrete!

You ask me to return

But I cannot

There are huge debts to be paid

But remember sweet-heart

The moon unites me with you all.

.

It was a podcast made by a young researcher on a local tribe and their dying oral culture. In her intro, she had talked of a gifted singer who narrated the agony of the uprooted.

His name was Mehto. Sans surname.

Anonymous. Last time, she met the famished singer, he was admitted into a municipality hospital.

I lost him from there. Concluded the researcher.

Nina fell in love again, this time with a popular image—an obscure singer; impoverished worker; a homeless migrant, untraceable, in the big, bad city of commerce.

She could understand the dualism of art — the simultaneous presence and absence of the creator.

An unseen artist becoming real through a distinctive voice.

THE CAMPFIRE

—There!

Silhouettes.

Sounds—growling, howling, roaring, barking, laughing—enough to unsettle urban imagination fired by a mysterious forest, on a wintry night. The campers, huddled around a merry fire, shivered by the strange.

Part of the *Gothic Trail*, they were there seeking adventure.

—Where? I cannot.

Rahul said, the usual skeptic.

—There.

Said the guide.

—Yes. I can see. Said Reema, adding: Glowing eyes. Edge of the lake.

The fire was continually fed. It leapt up high. The twigs burnt up fast in its yellow belly; the fierce flames, insatiable; warmth, comforting.

The bonfire lent a golden tinge to the faces. The shadows cast by the blaze were menacing.

—Look!

An outlined figure, shimmering.

The campers experienced a chilling sensation.

—Who is it?

The guide declared: Princess's Ghost!

—What?

—Yeah.

—Ghost?

—Every jungle has got dark denizens.

—Hmm. Do not believe.

Rahul said.

—I believe.

Said Reema.

Many colleagues nodded: There are dark forces.

Rahul smirked: *Imagining* things!

—You should not have joined the *believers*.

Said Reema: eyes red, speech, bit slurred.

The all-young corporate group from Delhi was getting excited slowly. The brooding forest and the strong wind added to the Otherness.

The lake glittered.

—Wherefrom comes the ghost?

Reema asked the guide.

—From the 18th-century fort.

—Why does she roam the night?

—She wanted to marry a commoner. When her lover was killed publicly, she jumped into the lake and died young and unfulfilled.

Rahul exclaimed: How romantic!

Rajesh countered: No. Real. These things happen.

—What about her lover?

Another camper asked.

The guide was silent. Then: Some folks have seen him also. Two separated lovers in different locations, on full-moon nights, pining.

—What if she pops up here?

Asked another woman.

—You will die of fright!

They laughed.

—Haunting in the outdoors!

Exclaimed Rahul.

They drank and ate supper. The moon shone on the trail leading to the fort. Trees swayed like drunken giants.

Wolves howled somewhere deep in the tropical forest.

—I can feel the spirits of the jungle.

Reema said.

—Oh! Revisiting the *Sea of Trees*?

Teased Rahul.

Rajesh replied: Even Aokigahara is real. There are realities outside human ken. We should not be dismissive.

—I am not disrespectful. Just stating my view.

Argued Rahul.

—Do not spoil the show! Rajesh admonished, every inch his senior in the office.

—Hush! Exclaimed Reema. I saw the spirits hovering behind the campfire.

—Where? Asked Rajesh.

—There.

They peered.

Fleeting figures in the damp air.

… A piercing cry.

Blood-curdling!

The group fell silent. The fire crackled. But the air underwent a change. Most felt evil lurking in the shadows.

—OK. I will check.

Before others could stop, Rahul ran down.

They waited.

…his loud scream echoed; desperate, chilling.

The men took up torches—to chase the scream, near the lake…

THE MONSTER SLAYER

...The trail goes to the cave of the monster. Slay your father-killer there.

The Old Seer to Kelly, the reluctant warrior.

The man with the golden locks and eyes of a poet would have rejected the challenge earlier but priorities change.

Then the nagging question: Why did it happen to me?

He was determined to punish the elusive beast.

As per the directions of the Wise One, young Kelly undertook a long and dangerous journey; the Wide River and stars, only compass. There were craggy mountains and treacherous paths; swift streams and fatal falls. A misstep—you are dead meat.

Last part, most testing!

The warning sounded true.

As Kelly approached the final trail, things grew strange. The cave did not look formidable or dangerous but rather beckoned!

An outside garden with a murmuring brook. The trees were in bloom and birds sang merrily. The seductive aroma of the exotic flowers and the soft breeze lulled the brave quester into sleep.

Waking up, he found himself tied on a rough table.

And a host that announced most cheerfully: Welcome, my lunch!

Kelly had never seen such an odd creature. The huge and unwashed hybrid stank badly. Bones littered the entire floor. The kitchen fires blazed, giving some light and warmth in that damp place. Dismal sight!

The giant reassured the victim gleefully: Do not be afraid. I kill my victims without pain. Only problem, I am bit slow for their liking.

Panic.

The monster got excited by the scent of fear: I thought you were brave but I can sense terror. Mortals! Easily scared!

Kelly was repulsed by the hollow laughter.

—Not fair! Kelly was calm.

—What?

—This uneven contest.

—Life! Never fair!

—You are philosopher also.

—I reflect. Observe things.

—Like?

—Humans love to invent their own monsters!

Kelly was astonished.

—A thinking man's monster. Not a complete brute!

—Fairy tales! Why do you create appalling images of the other species? Why this need for terrifying aliens?

—Because the unknown is dreaded. Part of evolution. Kind of processing threats in great images.

—Nice thinking, Kelly!

—Know my name?

—I can read the tattoo.

Kelly became quiet.

The fiend said: Monster is created to make you feel human, superior, master.

Kelly nodded.

They looked at each other for long.

— I like you, Kelly. Here is a game: Run for freedom. After an hour, I come after you. If you reach the border before, you win. Now run.

They agreed.

Kelly ran against the wind and crossed the border. Monster kept his word and let him live.

… Having survived the ordeal and returning home happily, Kelly remembered suddenly: Father killed by a beast-cum-cannibal.

He felt angry.

He was there to slay him, not escape.

Killing the giant, not easy.

Kelly knew he was to overcome fear and go back to the cave only.

There was no other way!

THE EXCHANGE

A quick exchange of smiles but could not escape him.

They sat on the sidewalk café. She wanted to catch the early-morning glory of the ancient city.

—I love the way sun paints Venice in gold! She exclaimed.

He nodded, adjusting the camera.

—I want the best shots. He said to the woman.

—Me, too.

The shoot began.

He asked her to tilt her head a bit against the bridge in the back. The Cathedral shone brightly. The waters sparkled. A gentle breeze blew across a slumbering street. The view was magical!

She walked with certain poise. Stopped. Bent a glance and smiled!

Setting his heart on fire! That Mona Lisa smile. The very quality was ethereal.

Then he realized it was not for him—but, maybe, for someone else. For a second, her eyes wandered, face lit up and lips formed into a grin, faint but sublime.

Out of the corner of the eye, he saw her fleetingly smile at a stranger clad in red T and blue denim, holding up a long stem of red rose. He smiled back. The tall rival stood inconspicuously among the American tourists and when the photographer looked back, the competitor vanished in air.

Afterwards, her face became serene.

Action in a jiffy!

Robert Browning echoed in an agitated mind;

...she liked whate'er

She looked on, and her looks went everywhere

Oh, sir, she smiled, no doubt,

Whene'er I passed her; but who passed without

Much the same smile?

Am I reading too much into a smile? He thought.

After some time, they went down to the bridge. She posed by pouting like Marilyn Monroe. She radiated joie de vivre that was infectious—waving at the kids, gondoliers; the Vietnamese waiters; Asian and Chinese tourists; nuns; old lady residents with small dogs; in fact, everything. Even he got affected and smiled at the world, forgetting a competing suitor.

She wanted to capture the famous spots.

Some poses were solo; others, in crowded plazas, train and bus stations, museums, and, the water taxis.

—I want a bit of Venice for posterity! She exclaimed, this beautiful French woman, hardly 24, with a lilting voice.

He followed as pet. Both sought immortality. He, from photography; she, modeling. Their worlds were different, yet converged in Paris apartment full of ambition where ethnicities hardly mattered.

While returning to the hotel room, she was a bit tensed, glancing back, often.

His peripheral vision registered these sideways movements of a person in perpetual rebellion.

For a sec, he saw a familiar figure but turning around, only a blur of action—a spot of red fading in a side alley.

They slept heavily after lunch.

When he woke up, she was not there.

A scrawled note: Sorry! Email the pictures.

Hit him hard!

Going through the pictures, he got the vital clue: In a frame, outer edge of the scene, a blurred figure, in red T, holding up a long-stemmed red rose...

THE GHOST OF R. KIPLING

Grandpa was a great storyteller. Here is his favorite:

In Shimla, I came across a hotel with a large sign: Discover history.

—What is the historic thing? I asked the portly owner, Wilson, the last Anglo-Indian family left.

—The Kiplings used to stay here in summers. We rebuilt the property. The Raj connection.

—Rudyard Kipling?

—Yes.

—Why demolition?

—It was in ruins. Remodeled the old colonial-style bungalow. Kipling enthusiasts visit us for that feel.

—OK.

The city was crowded with tourists. All hotels were full except this one, despite its good location, tranquility, nice garden and cheap tariffs.

Puzzling!

After checking in, I had this sudden creepy sense— of being watched by an *unseen* figure.

Spooky!

Never believed in the post-industrial mythology of haunting but something was definitely odd.

What was that?

I could not figure it out.

The answer arrived soon.

.

After a light dinner, smoke and stroll, I went to my corner room for the night.

And discovered R Kipling sitting in the chair, as a special guest!

Wanted to *scream*!

The author commanded serenely: Welcome to this encounter of a different dimension.

—Thanks. Why this conversation at this unearthly hour? I asked.

—You taught me for long.

I nodded.

—Chance brought you this place. The adepts are chosen for such Shakespearean trysts.

I smiled: Or Dickensian. Real haunting?

Rudyard: Writers never die. They get reborn. Resurrected by readers.

—Yes. I confirmed.

—Once you wanted to probe me. Go ahead.

I paused and then said: Yes, I do want to question you.

—Please do.

—Why did you paint the natives badly? The binary of whiteness and darkness? Civilized and savage? So predictable and overstretched. This supposed racial superiority of the West! Apes in need of salvation and light?

—Is it so? Give me the lines, angry post-colonial reader.

—Sure. I quote from that pathetic apology to imperialism, called "The White Man's Burden":

Your new-caught, sullen peoples,
Half-devil and half-child.

.

Take up the White Man's burden–
The savage wars of peace....

The ghost replied: What is wrong with that paean to the West and its civilization?

—Why not a Caliban in this insidious text? Counterfoil and argument?

—His trace is there.

—Very weak, in fact.

—Not everybody is Shakespeare. Besides, the age of empire is over.

—Sorry! The neo-imperialism is back and you are their latest icon.

He was mum.

I observed: Writers are either a presence or a specter. You have become a ghost that haunts the West and the East. Things change. The sullen peoples rising up against the empires everywhere. Half- devils against the full devils!

Silence.

—The country of your birth represented so poorly! Disgusting racialism!

He remained quiet.

—Savage wars, to be reversed. Retold. We reclaim, re-write R. Kipling!

He turned paler and then….

End it your way, reader!

OF A CYNIC AND SAINT

After the death of Pa, Mohan searched for a saint that could heal. He met few but got disillusioned—by an affluent style; roving eyes; long hair, beard; diamonds and luxurious cars. The thrones they sat; the distance between the gullible and idols clad in orange silks.

The disciples called these mortals, the gods walking the earth.

In India, they are the royalty—after cricketers and film stars. Over the years, some got arrested for wrong deeds, including assaults and rapes.

He lost faith.

Life caught on. Mohan had to look after a large family. Three siblings. Ailing grandpa. A mother working as a seamstress. He took up two jobs. Studied in the night college and after a hard struggle, got appointed as a lower clerk, in the excise department of the state government. The job was easy and the money was good. There were gifts and bribes. Over the years, he got his sisters married off and bought three apartments and cars. His arrogance and greed were limitless. For files cleared, money was demanded.

Rude. Corrupt but well protected due to strong network—typical government servant.

Hard drinker and womanizer.

The Godless man became a cynic. Only wealth and power mattered.

In the late 50s, bald and paunchy, while visiting his ancestral home, north of India, on a summer morning, Mohan Lal came across a familiar face: Harbir Singh, now dubbed as the Saint of the Haripur village. Harbir—the tall man in his 40s—looked serene and centered.

Harbir, a Saint?! The man with a past and no future.

Intrigued, Mohan made inquiries.

And the following account emerged:

After getting huge compensation for the land taken by the government for the expansion of the national highway, Harbir rolled in money; the former farmer started drinking, gambling and womanizing like crazy. He fought with everybody and chased women, getting beaten up by the relatives of the poor victims. He was beyond scruple and control—till sudden death struck.

His entire family got killed in a car accident while returning from a pilgrimage! He lost faith in a just God, renounced pleasures, grew a beard and withdrew from the *Sansar*.

The cutting of his *Peepul* tree and an unclaimed corpse further changed him.

He had watered the tree for long. The expansion of the road made the axing of trees necessary. When the fig tree fell, he cried like an orphan.

Next, he saw the dead body of a beggar, rotting in the open.

Then God called.

He hired an ambulance and did the rites on the banks of the Ganga.

A villager explained the strange metamorphosis—Last twelve years, Harbir Baba has been planting trees in a dusty plain being developed as the SEZ; transporting the dead of the poor in an ambulance bought for that purpose. Built an orphanage. Saint Harbir has touched thousands of lives and brought greenery to an urban hell.

A holy soul venerated by the entire region!

A stunned Mohan felt something moving, changing within…

THE CURSE

The last words: "Death, inevitable. My spirit will watch from this banyan tree, our home for years, dear Ka."

Inconsolable, he cremated her, on the bank of the Ganga, along with homeless others, living off the river offerings. The one-eyed vagabond had filled in cruel details: Foundling was adopted by the granny and named Ka because he sounded like a crow!

"Any idea of my parents?"

"Naw. You were dumped on the temple steps. Granny took you—like many such abandoned kids earlier. Fed the orphans by begging alms. Always nice and caring. Even educated some, this great soul."

No doubt, she was missed genuinely.

A grateful Ka had faithfully served the tiny woman. The tree was huge and both retired to its roots in the night. Two curs kept a watch over the rag-tag family. Granny was full of stories. She told Ka that the banyan tree was a living thing—and home to the undead.

"House of spirits?"

"Yes. Spirits reside in the banyan tree but never harm the good folks."

The teen was speechless!

"Every tree has got a native spirit. Never hurt trees. They are our kin. If you do, their curse visits you."

"How?"

"There is destruction around. Death follows in full fury."

Granny would daily offer water from the Ganga, tie a thread on its wide girth and pray. Ka was made to follow.

Their meager possessions—five cloth bags—would hang from its high branches. Nobody, not even the thieves, would ever dare touch them.

They were afraid of the fury of the banyan and the local spirits. Except for granny and Ka, nobody would ever sleep under its spreading branches, where owls and bats also frequented.

The banyan is sacred to the Lord Shiva! Very special.

Granny once observed.

.

Ka was sure the granny- spirit would protect him. So would the banyan tree. Once a junkie tried to assault him, early at night, but fled after seeing something in the air.

Ghost! He shouted and fled. Never seen again!
The legend of the tree—and of granny-spirit—grew. Villagers became reverential. And worshipped it.

Once, as per the account of another crazy addict, he saw the tree turning into the apparition of granny when he tried to snatch away one of the bags rumored to be containing gold and cash.

Ka was left in peace!

Then the skeptics arrived!

.

The city engineer declared the old banyan as a hindrance to their plans of the beautification and ordered cutting down of the tree bound in hundreds of red and white threads by women. Ka pleaded but was beaten by the corporation workers. It was killed brutally.

Beware of its wrath!

In the monsoon, granny's prophecy came true.

The Ganga rose in rage, destroying the bridge and everything.

Dredging by sand mafia, pollution, debris and plastic were touted as reasons of the choking of the river but Ka never believed this version.

The curse of a murdered tree was real!

As the rose-fingered dawn arrived, he could see the change around.

He had eagerly waited for the special hour when two opposites meet and separate. The night was long and tortuous. And, draining!

24 hours!

The doctors had predicted clinically. If the patient survives, chances of recovery are bright.

Awfully grim, the prognosis!

He had tiptoed to the ICU room and looked helplessly at the prostrate figure on the steel bed, all strapped up; the monitor flickering in the semi-darkness. The tubes were inserted inside the mouth; wrists bound; blanket in place. The figure, comatose, still.

A shrouded figure—mysterious, remote, beyond communication.

A life in balance!

Even prayers did not help!

Faith seemed to have deserted, when needed most.

Blank, inside-outside, he walked the corridors; pain on mute, seeing, yet un-seeing, like other attendants, majority sprawled in the narrow area meant for the relatives of such patients, admitted into a grey zone, where death and will-to-live battle in an uneven contest.

The post-Diwali Delhi sky was smoggy; air quality, very poor. Residents wore masks on the streets; a replica of some Hollywood film on dystopia being run in real-time.

Stars, hardly visible.

There was the stench of decay.

Hospitals always scared him!

Eerie feeling!

Subtle tension prevailed. The tension flowing out of an uncertainty— about the fate of a dear one, kept alive on a machine and by robots in white robes, un-smiling and gruff.

As the night slowly dissolved, he felt relief—visual, emotional, psychological.

After all, things might not be that bad!

The recovery is possible.

Miracles happen.

How light changes human perceptions, perspectives!

.

4.30 AM.

His mood lightened.

The gloom was dissipating.

The promise of a new, fresh dawn on the horizon!

.

5.05 AM

The sky turns magical. Few seconds, the dimness grows into soft mauve, then light purple, and, finally orange, deep and dark.

The firmament, live, electrifying!

...painted by Claude Monet: Impression Sunrise: Red, blue, gray—mixed up in blotches of colors, executed in short brushstrokes, forming a distinct sensory experience.

Marvellous!

The darkness fades; first light appears.

The divine vault radiates varied colors. The stars vanish. New day heralded by the resplendent goddess, called Aurora, Eos, Usha.

Be alive, up and early— to see the birth of a fresh world, at dawn!

He remembered Kalidasa:

Look to this day:
For it is life, the very life of life.
In its brief course
Lie all the verities and realities of your existence.
The bliss of growth,
The glory of action,
The splendour of achievement
Are but experiences of time.

For yesterday is but a dream
And tomorrow is only a vision;
And today well-lived, makes
Yesterday a dream of happiness

And every tomorrow a vision of hope.
Look well therefore to this day;
Such is the salutation to the ever-new dawn!

.

Reverentially, revived by the primeval energy, deity of daily change, he folds hands and begins chanting of the hymns in her praise; optimistic, positive, poised...

The reality sank in quick.

Not attentive, as they were practising Symphony No. 9.

The public service announcement (PSA) was repeated: Sorry to interrupt! Gunman has entered the building. Please do not panic!

The hall froze.

The PSA advised: Secure the doors. Hide. Cops, on the way.

The kids stood rooted; the music teacher's baton remained raised; colleagues and parents, incredulous!

Is it joke?

The PSA, in a grim voice, continued: Remain calm. We are monitoring the situation. Cops reaching within minutes.

They shivered.

How is it possible!

A gunman in their midst!

Just few seconds before, they were discussing the technicalities of the Ninth Symphony with the bulky conductor. The children, keen enthusiasts of classical music, following each instruction.

Not every day you come to play Beethoven in a suburban school. The members were excited by the prospect of a grand rehearsal. The "Ode to Joy" was the most important part.

The teacher said—Remember this Ode is as crucial today as it was in 1824! As inspiring and relevant as it was then.

The orchestra was all ears to the tiny Miss Anne who had learnt from a leading German school of music.

She continued: It is sacred, this Ninth and the Ode. Remember Beethoven was deaf! Still the maestro could produce such a time-defying music that is revered worldwide.

The class was intrigued.

They wanted to create history in a town deaf to music.

The group practiced daily and was to perform next week before a large crowd.

Each thought they were the Beethoven or Schiller, re-born.

Music meant everything to the select members.

It was a gateway to stardom and wealth—and escape from a small-town mindset and stasis.

Then cruel fate struck.

A gunman—out to kill!

The logic of a killer, beyond them.

.

The gun fire echoed in the corridor and shouts were heard. Somebody screamed.

The children huddled together. Some sat behind the chairs; others slid inside the silk curtains; the music teacher holding the youngest in arms and consoling by singing softly.

Adults hid in nooks.

Raw fear.

.

They heard someone banging hard with the butt of the gun.

More shouts outside.

Banging, louder this time.

Staccato firing of a round...more screams, in the bare corridor. Folks shouting in pain.

They were terrified inside the hall.

Open up! A demented voice commanded. Open up! Otherwise I shoot through.

Deathly silence... punctuated by loud sobs.

The smoke of the gun powder filtered in. Acrid.

A kid coughed badly.

Open up! If not, I shoot!

More firing, outside.

The sirens becoming louder.

The PSA cracked again: Do not panic! Remain calm!

.

The gun man enters, shouting: Stop! I hate music! Hate everybody! You must die.

Anne challenges: Why kill innocent kids?

The gun man laughs: Killing the Ninth-choir means killing the finest values.

Miss Anne counters: Hatred never works. Kill me, not kids.

The young killer aims at Miss Courage: OK.

Kids scream.

And then…

THE HOUSE WITH SECRETS

The house overlooked the gorge and the jungle in the distance. It nestled among trees—picture of pastoral tranquility.

—Why don't you buy this beauty? Sameer asked grandpa.

The old man replied: Nobody wants to own a house with bloody secrets.

—What?!

—Who would invest in a scary place?

—Why? Looks good! The facade is Gothic and in shape. Perfect with a garden and a well, except few rooms in bad condition and weeds.

Grandpa said: A house of horror!

.

The intrepid photographer in Sameer wanted to catch the colonial mansion in its full majesty.

Homes in varied shapes, sizes and moods were his main subjects. Took his camera and entered the property from a broken wall, as the front gate was locked, displaying the usual warning: *Trespassers be warned! Enter at your peril*!

.

Sameer loved to shoot the scenes in different light conditions. Fading light made the evenings, people and buildings, look melancholic, often tragic. Ruins were fascinating. They were the stories nobody wanted to hear. Histories receding. Narratives getting lost in the whirlwind of time.

The young photographer stepped over the broken beer bottles, cigarette and condom packets and leftovers of the orgies enacted within the heart of the imposing mansion, partially in shadows; an eerie silence prevailed everywhere.

Clearing the cobwebs and treading softly the dust of years, the athletic Sameer entered the corridors and shot the outer garden from the balcony; the balcony, from the garden with a marble fountain, dried and chipped.

The late afternoon sun could hardly penetrate the trees. The gloom was thick. Melancholic air hung over the deserted rooms and the courtyards, while the trees sang a unique dirge.

He went up to the third floor and took the pictures of the sprawling property. It looked normal.

No secrets!

Descending, he unsettled some bats that flew off and startled him by their screeching sound. Except that nothing odd.

Task completed.

Two hours. Hundreds of shots.

.

Over dinner, he said, grandpa, he found no secrets in the house. Grandpa said nothing but smiled.

The surprise was to come in the early night.

.

While going through the film, Sameer saw the most incredible thing!

In the ruins of the backyard, a figure in white stood out, clearly beckoning! An outlined female figure, slightly blurred but enough for a quick identification. The camera had got the figure.

He was taken aback!

He never saw a woman, while shooting.

Who is she?

A ghost?

*

Grandpa told him a tale of horror.

It ran like this:

The mansion and nearby fields once belonged to Robert Smith, a colonel in the British Raj. He led a life of debauchery. He was fond of the dusky *nautch* girls and often visited the brothels in the cities posted. His favouraite was Ruksana who often travelled with him and lived down the road in a cottage in Shimla. Her brother Mushtak was a procurer and goon. Smith became wild after few drinks every night and almost murderous, if displeased. Only Ruksana or Mushtak could have some calming influence on the *firangi* sahib. The soldier was often joined by other soldiers in the long summer evenings or short winter nights. They were entertained by the *nautch* girls and liquor flew freely. Although the superiors of the Raj frowned upon such dalliances, these souls hardly bothered about such niceties. They preferred the oriental prostitutes to the European ones.

We want to spread our seed among the heathens! That was their credo.

There were whispers among the British residents in Shimla that Smith loved Mushtak more than his sister. Everything was, of course, kept secret. Their affair was hush-hush.

*

Things changed dramatically when Smith's youngest sister came to visit him in India. She had heard a lot about India and its despotic rulers and barbaric practices. Once she heard a ghazal and fell in love with Urdu. Mushtak—the singer with a mellifluous voice and command over the court language—became her tutor. She learned a lot from that tall, strapping and dark man. Soon, she got besotted by his oriental charms and fathomless dark eyes. My Moor! She would sigh and the tough Pathan would melt before the Memsahib and act as her pet!

As their dalliance intensified, rumors spread fast. Smith hardly bothered about gossiping as he trusted his sister.

As the fate would have it, one summer afternoon, he came early and startled the unlikely lovers in her bedchamber.

The scene and the sudden shock unhinged him.

—If you can love an oriental, why cannot I? She asked her brother.

—You in love with a coolie? Low life?

—He is more refined than your comrades. Respects me. Devoted to me. Why cannot I love him?

—No. You cannot. He is heathen.

Smith was getting madder by the minute by her probing questions.

—Give me the reason. Why you keeping his sister as a mistress? Is it not unholy? Is she not heathen?

He did not answer her. Took out his revolver and shot the lovers in cold blood. When Ruksana came, he shot her also, shouting, whore!

Before dying, Rukasana said bitterly, your sister is a harlot! She seduced my innocent brother and others.

This made Smith insane. Shot the native servants. Buried the dead there on the property.

Chilling!

Grandpa smiled.

—What happened next?

—He was discharged by the courts on the grounds of temporary lunacy and moved to Punjab. Died there of syphilis or pneumonia or both.

  The property?

–Some cousin claimed it but went mad by the blood-curdling screams and the shots heard in the nights.

—Nobody interested now?

—No. The bodies were buried there. The ghost of Catherine haunts the cursed place.

—Why she beckoned?

—Because she wants her side of the story to be broadcast.

—Oh, the horror?

—The other side of the Raj.

IN THE NAME OF GANDHI

While recently covering the rough and tumble of the Indian elections for the Global News, Tapan Sinha found one of the most riveting human- interest stories of his career.

.

The wintry countryside looked desolate in the evening. Tapan and crew stopped at a Punjabi *dhaba* and ordered tea and *pakodas*. Some villagers gossiped over cups of Masala chai. Few minutes later, an old man entered. They touched his feet.

—Welcome, sir! The owner sounded reverential.

The man looked majestic in orange robes. White hair further enhanced his charisma.

The owner wanted Tapan to meet their Guru who inspired public respect and love.

Curious for a byte, the correspondent started asking questions about the elections and possible results.

The man said in impeccable English: These days elections are run on muscle and money. The independent India has junked the high principles of Mahatma Gandhi.

—Did you meet the Father of the Nation?

—Yes.

—How old were you at that time?

—I was 16.

—Now, how old?

—I am 96, thanks to yoga and a Gandhian lifestyle.

—Look younger than us!

The Guru smiled.

Where did you meet Bapu?

—In his ashram at Sabarmati.

—How did you reach there?

—Ran away from home.

—Why?

—Father served the British police. I did not like the servility. Wanted to serve my country. So I ran away from a home that hated the freedom fighters and called them traitors...

—Interesting! What happened next?

—I landed up in Bapu's ashram and stayed there for six months.

—How was he?

—Extra-ordinary. Out of this world. Without peers. True saint.

—Any incident that haunts?

—Yes, one incident that haunts to this day.

—Please.

He was quiet. Then: It is still painful.

—How? Please elaborate.

After few moments, the Guru spoke: Bapu was very punctual. Once, the lunch got delayed by one or two minutes only. Bapu, a stickler, did not touch the food, despite the pleading of the entire ashram. We felt miserable and guilty for keeping the pious man hungry. That day, nobody ate the lunch. We fasted and made it as a penance.

—Is it?

—Yes. We were devoted to him—like the rest of the nation. He was the soul of India. His words were sacred. Bapu was the noblest. I have not seen such a great man in my long life.

—Why did you leave the ashram?

—Well, he advised youngsters to complete the education and serve the mother- land from our homes. We did that.

As they were talking, the loud procession of a candidate stopped. The portly man stepped down from fancy car, surrounded by gunmen. Eyes blood-shot, the bejeweled man asked for their votes and then sped away, his men firing in the air, wildly.

The Guru looked grimly at the storm coming up on the distant horizon…

A VILLAGE OUTING

Damn!

Be real. Not virtual—24X7! Visit the village!

Resolution of 2017!

2018—about to end.

Resolution, unfulfilled. Whole year, lost!

New Year Resolution (NYR).

How fragile! You tend to toss them out first thing in the year that follows.

—Maximum shelf- life of an NYR is one week!

A shrink once claimed. He does not trust the species—like patients, the shrinks act weirdly. Might be wrong.

As Mukesh went through the diary- entries, he grew firm: Must honour the old NYR.

Three days left before 2019 gets ushered in. I must act.

Resolved to ring in the 2019 in the country with Subash.

In the December of 2017, Subash wanted him to visit his uncle's house in the village K, some 95 km away from Mumbai.

—You will see real paradise.

The ad executive had promised. The copy writer within a hard-boiled Mukesh got hooked to the idea of spending a night in a place that boasted idyllic charm for an automaton, desperate to flee on weekends, a living hell, vertical, gasping and restive.

Run away from the deadening routine. The tight deadlines. The office pressures. Stale gossips. Rivalries.

The bottom lines. New and impossible revenue goals. Mindless chase for profits.

—Is it? Retreat for soul? Not commercial stuff?

—Genuine. Not touristy. Ideal place to rewind. The experience enough to detox for a year!

—Semi-urban?

Subash said: Semi-urban, yes. The original lifestyle, intact. I often go there to get rejuvenated. Works for me.

—Sites worth visiting?

—The Titwala Ganesha Mandir.

—Any other?

—An old temple to Lord Shiva. Supposed to be made by the Pandavas during their exile. Historical.

—Some connection to the Mahabharata. Great.

—Yes. Would love it. The forest, rivers, tranquility. Balm to the soul.

—Sound like a tour operator!

—Selling the idea to a teammate. You can sell that to the boss for an ad-shoot. Nice natural location. Lot of greenery and stunning outdoor scenery.

They agreed to explore the area soon.

After few drinks, both decided to walk down to the nearby Parel railway station. As usual the road was packed with the automobiles. The sound deafened; the vehicle exhaust choked. Stray dogs barked. Hawkers occupied the pavements, with no room left for the pedestrians. The pair threaded their way in the controlled chaos.

10.30 pm. No let up in the manic speed of Mumbai, its mad honking; the acoustic violence and smoke drove asthmatic Mukesh crazy.

—Poison.
—What? Asked Subash.
—Slow poison. Cities are dead... nobody cares!

—Worst air quality. Winters are miserable. Delhi and Mumbai compete on that index.

The smog. Cannot breathe! Disgusting! —Killer air.

They hurriedly crossed an intersection, dodging bikers. December felt like May. The fumes stung like angry bees.

Irate Mukesh decided then: We leave tomorrow! —First thing in the morning.
That morning never came.

However, this time, they did.
Escape the megapolis.
Took the local train and the bus. Reached the desired destination. And stepped into another world.

A two-storied, red-bricked house, modest and self-contained: A Margo tree; basil plant; hand-pump in the corner of the open front yard; large airy rooms, minimal furniture; invigorating wind; yellow-white, preferred colors; cattle part of the collective existence.

A memorable event awaited the visitors. Farewell to a youth joining army. Emotional moment as the whole village had gathered for the departure. The young man beamed with happiness. He waved at the assembly and boarded the open jeep. His father smiled and said: Never show the back to the enemy, son. Do not be afraid to lay down your life for the country! You are our hero!

The village clapped as one. The recruit saluted. Band played the marital music. Folks danced. They showered petals.

Missing, such rousing nationalism in the metropolitan India. That afternoon got etched in his mind.

After delicious lunch, they strolled down to the temple of the Lord Shiva, built near the river. In the background, the forest loomed. Crossed a little stream to reach the modest structure steeped in faith. The old priest welcomed the visitors warmly— as if they were his kin. They prayed to the Lord and sat on the rude steps, feeling a strange presence.

There was solitude of a higher order.

With no madding crowds, traffic sounds, the enveloping silence and the cool breeze off the river refreshed them.

The birds sang occasionally. The trees whispered. The hills beckoned.

They went down to the clean river by crossing the fields and sat down on the boulders, the bare feet in the pure water, enjoying the scented air.

The priest joined the duo. Subash chatted up with him. The old man turned towards the newcomer and asked: Like the place?

Mukesh smiled: Indeed! You live here? The priest showed a house yonder: There. —Family?
—Eldest in the army.

—Oh! Everybody seems to be in army here.

—Soldiers and farmers are from countryside only.

—Yeah. Life is peaceful here.

The priest smiled. A hawk circled and swooped down on a fish down the river.

—It is tough! Urban India will not understand this.

—How?

— Many farmers are driven to commit suicide. The agrarian distress is wide- spread as a cancer.

—Right.

—Families suffer. Last week, a farmer hanged himself. We did not eat that day. Mourned him.

Mukesh nodded. He could feel the pain.

—Climate change makes lives harder. Stoics, we are. There is a huge disconnect between the two Indias.

Mukesh was amazed.

—You educated?

—In a way. Life, best teacher.

—Uncle Rao is M.Sc in agriculture. Informed Subash.

—What?

—Family profession, priesthood.

They finally returned. Everybody invited them. One extended family—the village.

Mukesh felt transformed. Purged of competition, negativity and isolation in that hard-working community.

Renewed!
That evening, he made latest NYR: Return visit to the village.

SOUL MATE

…remember June of 2018?

You quoted Pushkin that came as a surprise. I had come to know you in few hours of an unlikely rendezvous in a strange city; found you unpredictable. Enjoyed the swings, transitions.

Pushkin in Venice!
I was floored.
—You, a poet?
—No, you said. Love poetry.

The effect was tremendous.

Or, was it the setting?

The mood?

The person?

Or, all of them, as a combination?

Don't know.

One thing is certain. I got electrified by the lyrical fragment and the magic it unleashed.

Everything changed.

Solidity—as rendered in soft focus. The damp breeze grew scented; birds sang sweetly; the dull turned luminous, while we sailed:

Still I remember you appear

Before me like a vision fleeting,
A beauty's angel pure and clear.

How romantic!

Neruda quoted in Paris.

In the shadow of the Eiffel Tower, while taking a selfie; out of the blue, in a sonorous voice, a recitation that altered everything for me:

My love feeds on your love, beloved,
and as long as you live it will be in your arms
without leaving mine.

How much I enjoyed your company! Clear laughter. The frankness of the eyes and the voice. The natural candor.

The simplicity. The unpretentiousness.

Alive, in a deadening landscape.

We crafted dreams. Things moved fast. I was happy. The online dating games were exhausting.

Finding love, especially for a young immigrant, is difficult in a foreign city.

You were different.

Those last seven days!

We had become friends from utter strangers.

I wanted that status to change—from friends to lovers, and then, legally wedded couple.

Frankly, I had never bothered about arts. Never heard about these writers. I was not keen to know them further. My mind only understands figures, columns and calculations. Rest matters not.

But I was intrigued.

How did a computer professional know literature? Engineers are creative, somebody once told me.

I agree.
You discussed places. Music. Painting. Fashion. Street food.

My soul mate, I said.

My real love of life!

You smiled.

.

Over the weekend, you said you were OK with marriage.

That night, I could not sleep.

We decided to catch up in New York.

Things changed there.

You wanted more time.

I agreed.

The conversation grew short.

Then stopped.

After three weeks, I sent the following lines:

Love alters not with his brief hours and weeks
But bears it out even to the edge of doom.

Got a terse query: Since when an accountant turned literary?

After separation, I wrote back.

The answer never arrived.

Can people be so fickle in a market economy?

The hurt did not show. Immigrant friends told me of similar betrayals.

—We no longer believe in romance, they said. All crap!

I nodded. We were automatons battling hard for more profits.

Yesterday, I saw you in Central Park. You did not notice me, lost in your own world.

Quoting Petrarch, in a sonorous voice, over cell phone!

The forest called.

And the Beast.

From the hut, Raja looked at the mysterious swathe, right blend of darkness and light; the mobile chiaroscuro playing tricks. Home to odd beings—the giants, witches, elves, fairies. Daily talked to the fairies: requesting the airy denizens for a glimpse of Ma and Pa. The clouds, magically, turned into their smiling faces. The trees kissed a tear-stained face, the breeze whispered lullabies; the winged creatures made him fall asleep on the carpet of the leaves.

Grandpa demanded an explanation: I asked you not to venture into the forest. Why did you go?

— I love the place. The hut is lonely.

Grandpa yelled: Every mortal is lonely. Stay inside. The Beast lurks there. It prefers human flesh.

Raja nodded, waiting for the next opportunity.

*

Raja wanted to meet the Beast. On sleepless nights, heard roaring that curdled blood.

—What is a beast?

He once asked.

—Dangerous. *Wild*. Marauder.

—Eats kids?

—Yes. Raw.

—How he looks?

—Double-headed; eyes as smoking coals; swords as teeth and serpents, twin tongues!

The whiskered guy with red eyes should know. Feared for his deadly aim and fiery temperament. The cops once arrested him with the hides of leopards and lions. When Ballu returned from the jail, he was called the Devil. Frequented the forest, returning on each trip with the dead animals and tusks.

—How do you know?

Raja asked.

—I *see* him often.

—Can I *see* him?
—Yes. Inside the jungle. Near the Tiger Temple.
*

As he stood near the temple -ruins, he saw nothing. Finally, he gave up the quest. Returning, requested the mother fairy for the fabulous Beast.

The wish was granted.

… *The familiar roar…the monkeys chattered…the deer ran away…then, deep silence. A most magnificent animal appeared abruptly, out of thin air, looked at his seeker with kind eyes. The kid froze. The gaze was hypnotic. The striped animal strolled on the dirt trail and then vanished, walking like a royal; unhurried, graceful, its whiskers quivering in the cool breeze. As a departing gesture, it roared a gentle roar. The whole body of Raja and the jungle shook. It was a mystic encounter, changing him forever!*
*

Raja had never seen such a majestic animal—radiating natural power and energy.

He is not the Beast!

The Beast could have easily killed me! But spared my life.
*

Ballu promised to *show* the real beast.

Both went on a secret adventure.

After a long wait, Ballu said, *the Beast. It needs to be killed.*

Not the double-headed monster but the same splendid animal appeared nonchalantly into the view.

As Ballu took aim, Raja stopped him.

—Why?

—He is Not… the Beast.

—He is the Beast.

—No. Another species, different rules. Not even *wild*!

Ballu aimed again, a mad Raja fought the cold-blooded killer in that wilderness, screaming bitterly:

The Wild Beast! Wild Beast!!

IN THE CAFÉ

Each night I am reluctant to close up because there may be someone who needs the café.

—Ernest Hemingway

.

You would find him there only.

The waiters called it "the old man's table" and the regulars treated the informal arrangement as a reservation.

The business was slow; the well-lit and clean café was airy; clients stayed on, chatting or reading or staring sans any disturbance.

A cozy place with a good view.

The owner was deferential and ensured the old man was treated with kindness.

Every morning, the old man occupied that table only. The waiter would serve the coffee and withdraw.

The old man would be the king.

Nobody knew anything about the man. He hardly talked. His only companions were the tabloids. Read them with the attention of a student soon to appear for an examination. Both the waiter and the counter clerk—college-going males—watched him from a respectful distance.

The clerk remarked: This guy has got a weird habit.

The waiter asked: Tell me.

—The way he reads.

—How?

—Holding head in his hands, the way some chess players focus.

The waiter nodded.

—Totally engrossed in the piece. To the oblivion of others.

—Yep.

—It is a chessboard for him.

—Maybe, short-sighted.

—Suffering from a hangover!

.

One late morning, the clerk said, "Who is clicking pictures from outside?"

They both went out.

The clerk demanded the intruder: "What you doing, Mister?"

The bespectacled trespasser responded: "Taking pictures."

"Why?"

"I am a street photographer."

"What the hell is that?"

The photographer smiled: "I document the street life."

"What purpose it serves?"

"I capture the ordinary and turn it into the extraordinary. Sublime."

"What is sublime?"

"Forget that. Simply put, I capture common people, moods, and places and turn these into instant celebs. They become the Internet Immortals."

The duo got animated.

The waiter: "You make guys famous?"

"Yes. They get known the world over. Recognized."

"Show us your work."

He did. They were impressed by the range and skills.

"How do you do that?"

"It is an art and now don't ask, what is art?"

They laughed.

The duo invited the artist inside.

"Who is that man hunched over the paper?" The shutterbug asked.

"A regular."

"Interesting! What does he do?"

"No idea. Comes in, sits, reads, stares, pays and then leaves, without a word. "Sometimes, for hours. Reads the papers and mutters occasionally." The clerk said.

"Second home for him." Added the waiter.

"A well-lighted Café is a comforting place for many among the isolated, including writers. Enjoy the warmth and the reassuring presence." Replied the artist, "Reminds me of the old man with the dog."

"Who?"

"A character in Dostoevsky."

They stared.

"Do not ask me, who is Dostoevsky?"

.

They showed his picture, already a sensation in cyberspace. He was surprised.

"You *belong* to the world now, grandpa."

The man ordered for everyone, beaming for the first time.

THE RED BEACH

The beach that turns red in the evenings.

They loved that hour.

Father often went with him—to witness this red marvel.

The impressions are still vivid.

The beauty, ethereal.

How nature creates a daily miracle!

The sun going down.Scarlet orb, transforming the sky, earth and ocean into a red-covered reality, short, transient but uplifting.

Father would be awe-struck and remain silent as a worshipper in a sacred cove. Electric colors: Reds, pinks, oranges and yellows, swirling across the space.

Every object—dipped in red.

Cosmic painting in a staggering variety of the reds.

The right balance of intense and soft reds and yellows fires up the land, heavens, horizon and waters.

Enough to pin you down to a place the father-son came to christen as the Red Beach where gods come to play.

.

Father once remarked: A strange hour, this!

—How?

—Day is dying and night, birthing. Both merging seamlessly. Nothing beats it!

They felt overwhelmed by the enormity of the expanse; an al fresco collage, out on display for humanity that hardly bothers about such celestial works and the spiritual import of such elevated scenes.

Father often whispered: Mystical!

Prem, unable to grasp the profundity.

Under the palms, the pair sat and watched.

Father loved red. He painted the exteriors in red. The color changed the look of the house and turned it into the Red Palace, as the family called their tenement.

Prem once asked him: Why only red?

—It is very versatile color. Conveys variety of meanings. Symbol used by many civilizations from time immemorial. Unique. Same color, different non-verbal messages.

—Like?

—Courage. Change. Danger. Love. Sacrifice. Denotes fire and the sun. Aggression. Velour. Love. Marital status. Fertility. It goes on.

—Wonderful!

—Red stands out everywhere. Most warmly embraced by humanity. For me, it is sacred, as it was for many tribes earlier.

Prem could not understand.

Father smiled, saying: OK. Look up. That blaze there.

The red-pale-orange flames leaping in the sky.

—Now, look, there!

Gap in the empyrean heights, another reveal.

—There, Prem. The Mayan warrior. That gaunt face with streaks of scarlet- red.

The kid *saw* a face materializing before unbelieving eyes.

For him, Father was a magician.

—Yonder! The sky islands in the red sea.

—Yes.

—The Red Indian?

—Hmm! Ye-s.

—Good! You have got the blessed eyes.

—Which eyes?

—The eyes of the Ancients.

—Were they different?

—Yes. They saw what we cannot see.

—Is it so?

—Yes, son. Few mortals see like them now. Earlier, whole civilizations possessed that holy vision.

Prem lost him—again.

Father was often mysterious. But Prem obediently drank in his every word. He adored him, despite friends mocking dad's disability. And eagerly waited for his return. The lame salesman sold door to door, carrying a huge backpack on his bent back, a rod in hand. His voice had become hoarse, body weak but he never complained. Ate a simple lunch in the shade of a tree or a shop- awning and then moved on from one poor neighborhood to another, his smile intact. Father taught him an important lesson: Nature is God.

He made Prem respect nature.

Before leaving for work, Father dabbed the Basil plant with red and put a small dot on his forehead.

—Let God protect me!

It took many years for Prem to understand the significance of this gesture.

.

 Whenever in Mumbai, he makes it a point to visit the Red Beach.

His pilgrimage.

.

On the way to the Red Beach, he takes a water bottle and red color in a paper, keeps them in a cloth bag and reaches his fav place.

The connection starts.

The breeze is cool. On a working day, crowds are thin. He trudges down to the spot: His old shrine!

The evening is same—as it was earlier, in the company of Father. The Red Beach is same. The bend is there. At this strange hour, it is deserted. He sits on the sand and watches His hand paint the ocean, earth and sky in the same fiery reds.

Somebody is about to die somewhere; somebody to be reborn—in the daily cycle. As denoted by red.

Vintage Father!

Prem hears the old sounds again—a frail voice; the waves sing a dirge; the sea-gulls screech; the hoot of a fishing trailer in the distance.

And a scene that still haunts:

…they brought Father in an ambulance on a rainy evening. The sheet was covered in his fav red. When being taken out, the dried blood stains got washed by the furious rain. Father was kept in the wet front-yard, shielded by few black umbrellas. The slum-dwellers had come in hundreds. He stood motionless, unable to comprehend. Wet and shivering, his sobs getting mixed up in the torrential rain. The cops were kind but insisted the sheet be not unwrapped. Then they left. Rituals were done hurriedly. Prem had placed red flowers on the top of the bamboo stretcher and bid tearful farewell to a man, a constant companion for last 16 years of a happy life. Grandma had fainted upon discovering the still body of her dear son who had taken care of the invalid for many years. They cremated the dead near a swollen creek. Whole lives altered by an ensuing absence. Prem had become an adult overnight. He took odd jobs to look after the family and studied. On lonely evenings, he would come to the bend and listen to a voice, no more.

.

Prem's startup Red.com works with this message:

No rash driving! It leaves only orphans! STOP THE STREETS BECOMING RED.

He feels Father's presence around him.

He draws a father and son... watching the sun on a beach drenched in crimson...the waves wash the painting; the red-drawn figures merge with infinity—the ocean, on fire, at this hour.

VERBAL DARTS DO NOT HURT

"My mama always said, 'Life was like a box of chocolates. You never know what you're gonna get.'"

—Winston Groom

.

"You are my Forrest Gump."

Ma—years ago.

Roshan could not understand then.

At age nine, such cultural references made no sense, in a tiny town, north of India.

He heard her echo again, the previous day, in the call centre, when a co-worker said, "You remind me of Forrest Gump."

Roshan/Forrest was stumped. Past rushed back.

Ma.

Forrest Gump.

Roshan Singh.

Dadri, old home.

Delhi, new home.

How a feisty Ma and Gump had shaped up his forward journey, despite heavy barriers!

.

That Roshan was marked for life was clear right from school days. Ma once told a crying Roshan, "You need not cry but fight for your dignity. The world is brutal. It always was and will be. Stand up. Fight."

"How? I do not have your guts. They taunt me endlessly. Call me lame. Abnormal. If polio struck me, is it my fault?"

Ma smiled, "They are cowards. The brave never mock. These brutes ridicule His work. No option but to fight the mean bunch. God will take care of the rest."

"Does God exist?"

"Yes. He is different."

Another painful evening, Ma said, "Run, Gump-like."

Her parting words: "Look life in the eyes. Give it a run."

Repeated references made Gump mythical. Later on, he realized the man was pure fiction, made real by Tom Hanks and Hollywood money.

How Ma came to know about Gump? A typist with a criminal lawyer; a Christian married to a Hindu Rajput, an alcoholic who ran away with another woman, leaving her with an invalid and no money; the indomitable Ma fighting daily; this plain-looking woman, so amazing. She survived the beatings, the taunts, the insults of in-laws and relatives but never gave up or grew bitter. Once he asked her secret.

"Verbal darts do not hurt me anymore. Sticks and stones can break me but not words flung as missiles. This stoicism defeats enemies."

Her mantra for survival. His precious legacy.

Run!

The day the school opened and he came across Gulu, he hit the smirking bully's leg with his crutch. The latter howled. The gang ran away.

"See, what my lame leg can do. Next time, it is your head! My leg can split it open."

Gulu cowered and Roshan successfully completed his education from that Hindi-medium high school without ever being bothered.

All bullies are cowards!

Ma was right.

Roshan knew when to run and stop.

And fight the bullies.

Growing up in a poor and single-parent home was tough. Cousins or strangers laughed at his disability. A recruiter said thoughtlessly, we do not hire cripples!

Roshan had curtly replied, this mindset will lead to your becoming a cripple!

The courier company went bankrupt soon.

.

As he took a call from USA, he said quietly: Ma, Gump, thank you both, for your valued lessons.

REALITY SHOW, LIVE!

Marin Drive was full.

The breeze, a late-afternoon sun of December; Saturday crowds; linked couples gaze at the Arabian Sea; sellers of the cones of peanut and masala *chai*; strollers, and, few loners sit with dangling feet over the sea wall; crazy traffic on the arterial road; lonely-in-the-crowd feel—typical south Mumbai scene.

"Should we sit?" Mona asked and plopped down on a bench, vacated few seconds before.

"OK." Lisa also sat down.

"Good view. We wait here."

"Fine."

They were tired. Long commute, then a walk from the railway station. But the sea proved invigorating.

"Divine!" Exclaimed Mona, hushed tone.

"Come here often?" Lisa asked.

"Yeah." Said Mona. "Good for de-stressing in this mega city of more than 23 million wanderers."

"Hmm. Describes the city."

"Love the sea. Delhi does not have one. I come here on Saturdays and watch the sea. Spectacular therapy for soul!"

"Right. My Jodhpur is arid. Only dunes."

"I love desert also, Lisa dear. Are there princes around? Wearing swords, handle-bar mustaches and riding white stallions?"

Lisa laughed.

"Better you freelance for the Mills and Boon. Fantastic imagination!"

"Come on! Are not princess like that in Rajasthan? Feudal lords."

Lisa continued to laugh. "Things have changed dramatically. The royalty now sells nostalgia in their rented palaces for the elite and the foreigners looking for a bit of the exotic India."

Mona smiled. "You and your prosaic mind! Fit for number crunching only."

They grew quiet. The immensity of the blue sky and its reflection in a restive sea; the shimmering buildings of the far-off Nariman Point; the mobile mass of strollers on the promenade—pure seduction.

"Love Mumbai." Lisa said.

"It is scary also!" Said Mona.

"How?"

"Folks are detached. Stars on lonely orbits."

"The tragedy of every city these days. Nobody cares."

"Yes. Folks are getting indifferent. Atomized."

"We are part of the same culture. Do we care?" Lisa asked.

Just then they heard the sobs—loud, hysterical, body-racking, feminine.

A woman, in early 30s, was sitting on the next bench and howling— unusual behaviour in a public place!

Both the friends were taken aback. They forgot their own desultory discussion and turned around at the source of the loud racket, while other pedestrians, alarmed, gave the woman a wide berth.

Others got busy taking selfies of this sad human spectacle—a reality show, live, on a popular beach area.

The two girls, early 20s, gaped at a woman, weeping unabashed, hardly giving a damn to the world around.

She cried in bursts and then, in a continual spell… paused…and started afresh.

It looked odd: In the middle of a busy place, somebody cries her heart out to nobody in particular…and two women from the distant suburbs watch in numbed shock and total disbelief!

The vertical Mumbai, paved with gold, glitters in the weak rays of a pallid sun, apathetically!

People ignore the sight and increase their pace.

The Weeping Woman (WW) is non-existent!

.

Later on, Mona recalled the touching drama, on her blog:

The first thing I noticed about was her dress. It was costly, top brands only; Western, well- color-coordinated. She looked elegant. The sun goggles placed middle of the head. Everything about her spelt class. Tall, slim and fair-complexioned. Model-like. Not an impoverished girl, vulnerable, who can dissolve in a public place. This puzzled us. She continued to sob, stop and sob serially. Although some guys lingered around her, yet nobody dared go and ask her the reason behind the outburst.

They did not have the nerves, maybe.

We too thought we should leave but Lisa decided otherwise: "Come on, Mona. We should not walk out. She needs help. Let us go and find out."

Without thinking, we went to her, with Lisa in-charge.

She sat down near her and asked quietly, "Hi! Can we help, please? What is the matter? Anything we can do for you?"

The WW was stunned by our sudden appearance and concern.

She blinked, mouth open. Fluttered her lashes and then cried at the top of her voice as if she had found a lost kin or some kindred spirit.

Lisa held her hands.

WW tilted the bobbed head and rested it on Lisa's shoulder. Crying bitterly.

After several minutes and a soft pleading by Lisa, she relented and opened up in bits.

What emerged was a heart-rending urban story of a broken heart.

The lady was in her early 30s. Worked as a media assistant in a production house.

"Some days are not perfect. It is one of them." She said.

"How?" I asked.

"Nothing seemed to work in your favour."

"Like?"

The woman slowly said, "Morning, I get the news that Ma has been diagnosed with breast cancer. Devastating! My best friend gets admitted into the ICU. I cannot believe. Then, most surprisingly, I lose my job in the post-lunch hour. Ultimate blow! Get called by the bald boss. He asks me to leave the keys with him. Like that. No explanation. Nothing."

We are now genuinely shocked.

"Indeed!" I exclaim. "Not fair."

The woman becomes quiet. Then: "With a messy divorce on, the downsizing was the last thing. Felt miserable. Angry. Something snapped. wanted to run and hide some place and bawl. Office and home, no options. Decided to come here. Had found my love on this beach. The man with a baby face… a monster in reality. Overcome with sadness, I unburdened, in an anonymous place, where I will not be noticed."

Lisa said, "Sorry! Never meant to intrude but felt we must help a sister in distress."

I nodded.

She smiled through raw tears.

"Take care. God bless." We stood up.

She hugged us spontaneously and said softly, "Thanks, my dearest sisters! Never believed God sends His angels in the form of total strangers—to share your pain, in unlikely spots.

And thus, HEAL you up. You are noble. Saved a life toady by talking. God bless."

We shook hands and left, strangely transformed.

ON A HOT DAY SOME STRANGE KINSHIP

The heat is killing me.

Inside the car, the heat of early May does not cause much discomfiture; as it does outside, on the road near a busy railroad station, in the central suburb of Mumbai, on a working day, full of twists.

Wait at the bus stop!

The WhatsApp command that you ignore at your own peril.

Have to wait.

The mid-day traffic horrible. No room for pedestrians. Usual honking and strays. Drivers jump and overtake madly.

The heat of a coastal city. Humidity turns it into a ruthless killer.

A dusty wind hits---bees stinging!

What the hell!

The enforced wait.

Watches the scene, otherwise a daily blur, in a car drive. The mélange of cars, bikes, auto rickshaws and buses, unregulated, chaotic. The City never stops---rain or sun shine.

He glances at the watch and curses.

The local train has got late.

The heat intensifies further.

Cannot take it any longer, direct exposure to the fierce sun. I might faint or get dehydrated or get a stroke.

Who cares?

The cap does not protect.

Any shade nearby?

None, as expected. They never plant trees here, only uproot for widening.

Few minutes at the roofless bus stop and it is hell---roasted alive.

The tar has melted under the 44 degrees. The heat from the surface, unbearable; it singes the skin.

The high temperature prompts him to see certain things he never saw during car-commute.

The other side of the heat and working city.

A stunted tree!

The lucky survivor!

It offers a welcoming shade.

Big relief!

He cannot name it but he realizes its silent value.

Trees chopped down. Concretization. Rapid urbanization. Garbage. Choked rivers---recipe for disasters.

The dusty tree acts as a frayed umbrella.

He looks up and nods.

For a second, he thinks he saw it nodding back as a buddy!

The searing wind refreshes!

Adjusting the goggles, he looks around as a flaneur...and *discovers* an *old man* selling cucumbers few feet away.

On a small, hand-driven cart, the cucumbers are neatly arranged and sprinkled with bucket- water by the seller---lean, short, head covered in a polythene bag. The assorted goods tempt--- green, fresh, cheap.

The heat does not bother this man!

Strange!

The old peddler is at the intersection, where traffic is maximum- --pedestrian and vehicular. Few workers give orders. The old man becomes animated, hands move fast, sprinkle salt and lemon on the cut pieces of the long cucumbers, and then placed lovingly on newspaper pages, as wraps for the hungry mouths.

Customers gone, the old seller assumes the earlier pose--- upright, stock-still, one arm stretched over the goodies, a frozen statue.

His grit, demeanor and stoicism, impressive.

He beats the sun!

The street dog!

Strays repel.

He wants to shoo off the mongrel but somehow, stops.

Looks into the brown eyes set in a sunken body. He smiled and dog wagged its tail.

Both stood there under a smiling tree...

THE CLOWN THAT WAS NOT

The baby was bawling and young mother could not comfort it in the crowded compartment. Maybe the heat and dust of the desert added to its discomfiture. It kept on crying, the shrill notes drowning the other voices, as the train hurtled down.

"Why cannot you make it quiet, woman?" asked her bewhiskered and tall husband, his large head encased in a saffron-colored turban. He carried the long sword and the proud demeanor of a warrior. The imposing personality, the *khol*-lined eyes, fierce and glittering, left us in awe. The man carried himself in dignity and sat alert and erect. Often, his right hand twirled long whiskers. Nobody could hold his stare for long. His wife—in her 20s—cowered in the corner seat, face averted, trying to make the baby sleep but to no avail. The un-reserved compartment was full of the peasants and workers, every inch taken by the sweating bodies. Even the passage to the toilet was occupied by families.

"Try harder, woman!" The warrior barked. The woman in veil tried harder. The baby cried louder. The man glowered at her and the baby, upset by the bawling—and, maybe, the inability of a wife to execute a stern command.

The howling continued for minutes.

The warrior was getting annoyed. The woman was in panic— and the baby unstoppable. As the husband tried to snatch the child from the lap of a hapless mother, a calm voice rang out: "Hey, kid! Look here!"

Not only the baby but we all looked at the source of this majestic command that made the chatter die down in that car, almost on fire under an angry sun. The dunes slipped by and the bleak land continued to rise and fall for miles. Nothing but golden sand!

Our eyes stung and burnt and uncovered face and skin got singed. Now quiet, the fellow passengers looked around and saw the new entrant into a familiar Indian family drama seen often in the public places like airports, bus and railway stations.

It was an unlikely figure: A short guy, on the opposite wooden bench, now talking to the baby. He snapped fingers, sang in a sing-song voice and, in a jiffy, took out some items from an old bag and put on a red nose, a crimson wig, white beard and multi-hued cap.

The transformation from being an ordinary man into a clown was complete in an instant.

The baby got distracted by the startling change. He clapped, nodded and sang a ditty in a sonorous voice. The baby started laughing—and soon fell asleep, to the relief of the spectators.

"You are a great guy!" The husband remarked. "Thanks. His cries were making me sleepless. The kids of warriors do not cry."

His wife also nodded silent thanks. Her big eyes conveyed a sincere gratitude to the strange savior who smiled happily.

The baby was in deep sleep, oblivious to the racket around and the clatter of the wheels and the hot winds and the dust that filtered in through the slits of the shuttered windows.

"Please! It is my lifelong passion. To make folks smile through tears. Especially, children. These are special gifts of God. My way of worshipping Him through this humble service to His creation." The clown said in a pleasant tone, kindness radiating a weather-beaten broad face.

We all nodded in admiration.

"You are kind man." Somebody remarked.

"And a wonderful soul!" Another exclaimed.

The clown beamed.

"Are you working in some circus?" asked a young farmer, wide eyed.

"A long story, sir." The clown sighed.

"Tell me your story, please." The warrior requested.

"Please. The journey is long. It will kill the tedium." The farmer requested.

"OK." The clown relented. "Listen."

An amazing tale of courage, grit and nobility, in a big circus run by a selfish tyrant, greedy for profit only.

A tale of sacrifice, pain, humiliation, torture and dedicated community service.

Here, his story in his words:

I never intended to begin a career in a circus. Born in a little village in Nepal, I was recruited by an agent of the *Rio Circus* who promised heavens for my six siblings and poor parents and at the age of eleven, I left home for a new world of travelling circus. Over the years, I realized that my limp, seven fingers and squint eyes were the main reasons for my selection as a clown in a place full of freaks and exhibited before a callous public as odd entertainers—seven-feet giant; a hirsute man looking like mini gorilla; a two-feet dwarf; Siamese twins; a pair of albinos and pygmy hunters, among others. It was a strange place! The owner called the Boss was initially kind and supportive but later on, in order to attract more crowds, tried to model himself as the new-age avatar of P. T. Barnum. "I am the greatest showman on this part of the earth! Ha! Me and my menagerie! The more the freaks, the better the revenue. But I will share the profits with you guys. I will balance you with animals. A big family of entertainers." We all nodded. "I will take you to Russia and America. Mine will be a unique show on the planet. I will add music, dance, mimicry, acting and shows by the freaks and animals. A three-hour family package." The Boss brought some failed artists from film industry and animals from illegal markets. Bribed the authorities. Managed the media outlets. Within a decade, his circus became the top draw. Whole towns rushed in for his daily three shows. The house was always full. He took care of everybody as his family but soon international recognition for his skills and managerial ability made him go mad. He became ruthless megalomaniac. He wanted to conquer the world. And our nightmare began!

He would beat us and the poor animals for minor mistakes. Abuse the women. We got terrified of him, especially when he was drunk and nasty. He would make us perform, even if we were not well. Did not pay us for months and if anybody tried escaping the hell, chained and starved the fugitive. During the days, he was an angel, especially before the public and nights, a monster in search of fresh human flesh. Once I saw him naked with the wife of his trusted friend, the ring master. He pointed a gun at me, saying softly, eyes cold: "Tell this to anybody and you are dead meat, you hideous clown!" The woman openly laughed and added: "Such a repelling figure!"

It totally devastated me—the humiliation of a popular clown and the betrayal of friendship and trust. The Boss was like that—unethical, pleasure-seeking devil. I began hating his dark side. The wife of the ring master would jeer at me, whenever we met. I came to hate that slut also. Then, one day, he seduced my sweetheart, a kind girl, and told me afterwards, this Boss, before the entire staff, in a drunken stupor: "Your girl says you are hopeless in bed. Ha! She is my new slave!"

I felt like revolting. During one of the stormy nights, I ran away. Few miles down the swamp, his goons caught me and thrashed me before the circus staff. "Next time, kill this bastard!" The Boss yelled, almost hoarsely. Everybody laughed at me, so degraded each of us had become, enjoying the misery and humiliation of a fellow victim and sufferer and driving sadistic pleasure out of the misfortune of a friend or colleague! It saddened me further—my alienation was complete. What was earlier a source of joy for me—making the lonely, sick, kids and old persons laugh by my antics, every day for years—became a painful burden. Circuses these days are positive and places of joy and humane treatment of certain animal species but those days were more primitive and brutal. The Boss came to believe he owed all the creatures and could do what he wanted to do without any sense of scruple or shame. He bent everybody to his will and desire and dissidents were whipped or thrown out of his running caravan into wild gorges or mad rivers.

So that day, he shamed me. Something died within as the family mocked me.

Except the Gorilla!

At this point, the listeners asked in unison, Gorilla? He smiled and nodded. Then resumed the gripping tale— the compartment as his audience.

Yes, Gorilla!

Over the years at the *Rio Circus* I had come to develop a bond with the animals and learnt their ways and languages. Among the menagerie, the closest was the Gorilla. I would chatter with him on dull nights or mornings, when the family slept.

"Why sad, human?" The Gorilla asked.

I began crying before his huge cage kept in a corner of the barricaded property, outside the city.

"What happened?"

I told him of my public insult and humiliation. Of my wish to take my life rather than suffer daily.

He thumped his chest lightly and then grunted, "Human! Your master is brutal like rest of humanity. You and few others are an exception. Look at me. Has put me in prison. My fate is worse."

This simple revelation prompted me to see him—and other innocent animals imprisoned in horrible enclosures or cages in that travelling circus—in a totally different light. The brutality, sheer torture and misery of these gentle souls made me angry.

"We are not to be put on display like exotics before a crowd that cheers our misery. We are different species but that does not grant the Boss to treat us as inferior, as slaves."

I was surprised by his smart observations.

"Look, you can get even with that mean human!"

I looked at the Gorilla, "How?"

He said, "Easy. Set me free. Release me from the cage and then see."

And I immediately *saw* his point!

We all grew quiet; the compartment became one in asking the clown, "What happened next?" He kept silent. Drank water from an old bottle and then told us rest of the story.

On the appointed night, when moon was low and storm clouds were there in an ominous sky, I unleashed mayhem by releasing the Gorilla and other animals kept in chains or small box-like cages, one by one. The Gorilla tiptoed to the main tent of the Boss and emitted a blood-curdling laugh. At that point, clouds came and obscured the moon. Rain began in angry torrents and thunder struck. The laughter of Gorilla began rising up and he tore down the grand tent. The Boss got scared by the towering gorilla. He tried to train his gun on the beast but the gun and the man stood no chances against an infuriated gorilla. He flung the gun and the Boss against the cages of the tigers and lions and then ran after his trainer. It was a mad scene—animals chasing their tormentors in rain and gloom, the latter scattered and running blind. The animals tore down the circus. Then they ran down the streets of the small town on the edge of a deep jungle. The combined roar of the released animals—wounded and broken in spirit, chained and beaten for years—shook the houses. The tigers and lions growled and elephants trumpeted and thunder clapped. The town shook. The cops hid underground. I rode with the animals.

The Beasts had taken over!

Next morning, the free animals roamed a deserted town. The townspeople were shut inside. Gorilla saved a kid who had fallen from a balcony and placed it back on the steps of a panicky home. Then, the beasts retreated into the jungle.

"What did you do afterwards?" The warrior asked.

"Oh! Never joined any circus. Became a travelling clown. My mission: to make sad folks smile. The world needs clowns."

Everybody clapped and even the baby, now awake, smiled…

Ps-Fs :: Sunil Sharma

Paco's Atlas And Other Poems
By John Thieme

India as an IT Superpower
Anurag Sharma

अनुरागी मन कथा संग्रह :: लेखक: अनुराग
शर्मा

आग से अंतरिक्ष तक :: अज़ीज़
राय

Basic Hindi 2 Workbook :: Sonia Taneja

A few other books from Setu Publications, Pittsburgh, USA

AUTHOR-BIO

Sunil Sharma is Mumbai-based senior academic, critic, literary editor and author with 20 published books: Seven collections of poetry; two of short fiction; one novel; a critical study of the novel, and, eight joint anthologies on prose, poetry and criticism, and, one joint poetry collection. He is a recipient of the UK-based Destiny Poets' inaugural Poet of the Year award---2012. His poems were published in the prestigious **UN project: Happiness: The Delight-Tree: An Anthology of Contemporary International Poetry**, in the year 2015.

Sunil edits the English section of the monthly bilingual journal *Setu* published from Pittsburgh, USA:
http://www.setumag.com/p/setu-home.html

For more details, please visit the blog:
http://www.drsunilsharma.blogspot.in/

www.ingramcontent.com/pod-product-compliance
Lightning Source LLC
Chambersburg PA
CBHW052012240626
47153CB00008B/2838

* 9 7 8 1 9 4 7 4 0 3 0 4 8 *